Cristina Kim
♡

Courage
in the
Classroom

by Cristina Kim
Illustrated by Luke Fimio

ISBN: 978-0-9921349-9-0

Printed in the United States of America

Written by Cristina Kim and Ange Friesen
Illustrated and designed by Luke Fimio
Edited by Linda Pruessen

Wisetree Media, Publishers
Canada

www.mybestfriendinni.com

This book is dedicated to all children.
May your Inni be with you always.

Introducing...

Inni

"I'm your intuition and your guide to being a real superstar! I'm always there for you!"

Love

"Hi my lovely friend! Do you love everything mushy gushy lovey dovey like me?"

Honesty

"I always tell the truth and nothing but! I am about being honest every single day."

Kindness

"Being kind is an everyday, all the time thing! I'm a super caring friend who puts other people first. Always."

Harmony

"I play really well with others. When people get along, it's music to my ears."

Generosity

"I love to share everything. You need a hug or a friend to hang with? I'm here!"

inni, friends & frenemies

Courage

"No matter what, I stand up for what's right. Just call me and I will be there."

Bully

"I make myself big by making you feel small. Being mean gets me what I want!"

Liar

"Who needs to tell the truth? Not me! I'll say anything to get what I want, and I'll even lie for it."

Selfish

"I'm all me, me, me and I don't care about other people's feelings."

Envy

"I'm NEVER happy. Everyone always has better things than me! SO unfair!"

Hi, I'm Max. I'm going to visit my best friend Inni. Why don't you come along?

Inni is my intuition. Whenever I'm not sure what to do, Inni is always there to help.

But right now, it's Courage who needs Inni's help. Let's get to my Inniverse and see what's going on!

Courage loved mornings. He loved waking up with no idea of what might happen. Anything was possible. Each day was different. But this morning was differently different.

Everything was heavy. His head felt heavy. His whole body felt heavy. His steps were extra heavy. But the heaviest thing of all was his backpack.

Inside was a note. "Please see me," it said.

Courage hadn't done well on his last quiz. Again. And now, that one sheet of paper, signed by his teacher, was making his backpack feel a whole lot heavier.

Courage did *not* want to go to school. As each day passed, things got harder and harder. No matter how much he tried, he couldn't help but feel like a big dumb rock that no one wanted around.

Honesty and Courage walked to school together every morning. And sure enough, Honesty was waiting at their spot.

Courage couldn't tell his friend that he was dreading school. Honesty would *never* understand. School came so easily to him. And besides, Courage was supposed to be brave. And courageous! He couldn't show his fear.

"Hey, Courage," Honesty called out.

"Hey, Honesty," said Courage. "How's it going?"

"Forget about me," Honesty said. "What's going on with you? You look terrible!"

Courage shrugged. "I'm fine," he said. Courage set off towards school, leaving Honesty to follow.

When they arrived, though, it was Courage's turn to lag behind.

"Aren't you coming?" Honesty asked.

"Um ... I forgot something," Courage said, nervously. "Go ahead. I'll catch up."

Courage wasn't at school all morning. At recess, Honesty looked around for his friend, but Courage wasn't there.

Something was definitely wrong, but Honesty didn't know what it could be. He wanted to help Courage, but how?

As he was thinking, a familiar fuzzy feeling tickled his tummy.
Inni had arrived.

Honesty was so happy to see her. "Inni, something isn't right with
Courage. We walked to school together this morning, but when we got
here, he ran off. I'm not sure what to do."

"I think I know where I can find him," Inni said. "You go to class.
And don't worry; everything will be alright."

Deep in the Inniverse Forest, Courage sat in a quiet shady spot. It was his favourite place, perfect for being alone.

Courage couldn't go back to school. And it wasn't just because he was scared to talk to his teacher.

Everyone else got way better marks. They were always told how smart they were, and they seemed to *have fun* when they were there. That never happened to him.

A gentle breeze rustled the leaves overhead, and Courage felt a rumbling in the deepest part of his belly.

"Hi, Inni," he said.
"It sure is nice here," said Inni as she settled in next to Courage.

"I know I should be in school," Courage said.

"So why aren't you?" asked Inni.

"I don't like it there," Courage said, sighing. "I'd be happy if I *never* had to go back."

Inni sighed too. "Did something happen?"

"No. Nothing ever happens. That's my problem,"
Courage explained. "Nothing makes sense to me.
And the teachers just get annoyed."

2x5?

8+7?

5x3=...?

20-8=...

Courage started to cry.

"It's okay, Courage," Inni said, floating closer to her friend. "Everyone learns things differently."

"But I can't seem to learn things *at all*," Courage said.

Sob..

Sob....

"Oh, Courage, that's not true. I've seen you learn many things. You just need a little extra help sometimes."

"No one wants to help me," Courage said.
"They wish I wasn't there."

"I *know* that's not true," said Inni. "In fact, Honesty is really missing you right now. And I bet your teacher has some ideas for how to help."

Courage sniffled. "She wants me to come see her," he said. Inni smiled. "So why don't you talk to her?"

"What if she says I'm hopeless? I'm too ..." Courage's words trailed off. "Scared," he finished, in a small voice.

Inni hugged him. "It's okay to be scared."

"But I'm Courage!" he said. "I'm not supposed to be afraid of anything!"

"You *are* courageous, Courage," Inni said. "No one else would be brave enough to come so deep into this forest.

"But being courageous doesn't mean you're never afraid," she continued. "Courage is doing the right thing even when you are. It's not being courageous if you're not at least a little bit scared."

Swoosh!

Courage looked at Inni. He knew she was right.

Inni spoke again. "If I come with you, do you think you could talk to your teacher?"

"I think so," he said.

Courage and Inni arrived at the school just in time for Study Hall. Inni smiled encouragingly at Courage. He took a deep breath and walked through the door.

Inniverse Elementary

After school, Honesty wasn't sure whether he should wait for Courage. He hadn't seen his friend all day. He was just about to head home when a voice rang out across the yard.

"Hey, Honesty!" Courage called.

Inniverse Elementary

rumble

rumble

23

"Courage! Where have you been?" Honesty asked.
"Are you okay? I was kind of worried!"

"I'm okay." Courage laughed. "I was just feeling a bit out of sorts."

Courage thought about what Inni had said. He took a deep breath and made himself explain. "I was scared. I've been having some trouble in class, and Ms. Knowledge wanted to see me. I was worried."

24

Courage glanced at Honesty, hoping his friend wouldn't think he was too silly.

"You should have told me!" Honesty said. "I can help! We can study together after school any time."

"Thanks, Honesty. That would be great," Courage said. "Ms. Knowledge is going to help me too."

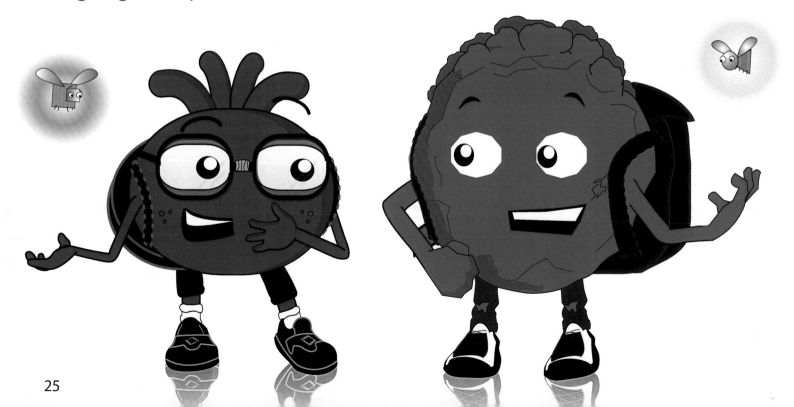

The two friends walked home together. As usual, Honesty talked the whole way, and Courage listened to his smart friend's stories and ideas.

Courage's steps got lighter and lighter as they walked. By the time he got home, he could barely feel his backpack on his shoulders.

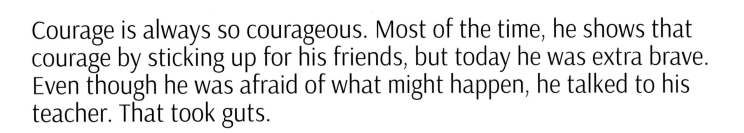

Courage is always so courageous. Most of the time, he shows that courage by sticking up for his friends, but today he was extra brave. Even though he was afraid of what might happen, he talked to his teacher. That took guts.

Sometimes I have those same feelings. I get worried and nervous and insecure. When that happens, I want to run away and hide, just like Courage did at first. But I almost always feel a lot better when I face my feelings head on.

You know what helps? Inni! She's always around when I need her. And when I need extra help, I think of Courage. Then I know I can do it—whatever it is.

I hope your Inni can help you the next time you're a little bit nervous—at school or anywhere!

See you next time!

All mybestfriendinni books are available in print on Amazon,
or for free download at www.mybestfriendinni.com.

baby max

Your Very Own Magical Place
by Cristina Kim Illustrated by Jennifer Pratt
a mybestfriendinni story

inni & friends

Everyone
Longs
to
Belong
by Cristina Kim
Illustrated by Luke Finto
a mybestfriendinni story

Bully is
as
Bully Does
by Cristina Kim
Illustrated by Luke Finto
a mybestfriendinni story

Kindness
Finds
Her Voice
by Cristina Kim
Illustrated by Luke Finto
a mybestfriendinni story

Courage
in the
Classroom
by Cristina Kim
Illustrated by Luke Finto
a mybestfriendinni story

Generosity's
Backpack
by Cristina Kim
Illustrated by Luke Finto
a mybestfriendinni story